Notes to Parents and Teachers:

At this level of reading, your child will rely less on the pattern of the words in the book and more on reading strategies to figure out the words in the story.

REMEMBER: PRAISE IS A GREAT MOTIVATOR!

Here are some praise points for beginning readers:

- You matched your finger to each word that you read!
- I like the way you used the picture to help you figure out that word.
- I noticed that you saw some sight words you knew how to read!

Book Ends for the Reader!

Here are some reminders before reading the text:

- Use picture clues to help figure out words.

- Get your mouth ready to say the first sound in a word and then stretch out the word by saying the sounds all the way through the word.

- Skip a word you do not know, and read the rest of a sentence to see what word would make sense in that sentence.

- Use sight words to help you figure out other words in the sentence.

Words to Know Before You Read

book

draw

friend

gym

jump

jump rope

partner

sit

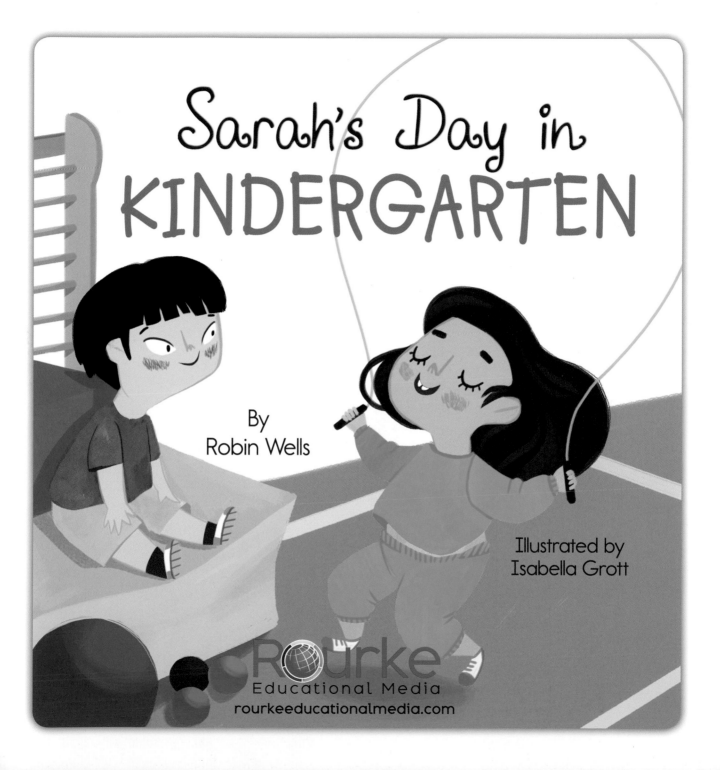

Sarah's Day in KINDERGARTEN

By
Robin Wells

Illustrated by
Isabella Grott

Rourke
Educational Media
rourkeeducationalmedia.com

"Good morning, Jimmy! Good morning, Sarah!"

"Please sit with your partner," said the teacher.

"We are going to jump rope."

"I can jump ten times!" said Jimmy. "I can jump more!" said Sarah.

Where are they?

They are in gym class.

"We are going to read a book," said the teacher.

"This story is funny!" said Jimmy.
"Let's read more books!"
said Sarah.

Where are they?

They are in the library.

"We are going to draw best friends," said the teacher.

"Who are you drawing?"
asked Sarah.

"Guess who she is," said Jimmy.

"I know! That is me!" said Sarah.

"Yes, Sarah. You are my best friend," said Jimmy.

"Jimmy, you are my best friend,
too!" said Sarah.

Where are they?

They are in art class.

Book Ends for the Reader

I know...

1. What did Jimmy and Sarah do first?

2. Where did Jimmy and Sarah read a book?

3. Who did Jimmy draw a picture of in art class?

I think ...

1. Have you ever jumped rope?

2. Who is your best friend?

3. What kind of stories do you like?

Book Ends for the Reader

What happened in this book?

Look at each picture and talk about what happened in the story.

About the Author

Robin Wells is the mother of two who lives in sunny Florida. She has authored over 30 books for children and young adults. She doesn't really have a favorite subject or topic to write about. They are all special to her and she often enjoys writing them with the sun in her face and her feet in the sand.

About the Illustrator

Isabella was born in 1985 in Rovereto, a small town in northern Italy. As a child she loved to draw, as well as play outside with Perla, her beautiful German Shepherd. She studied at Nemo Academy of Digital Arts in the city of Florence, where she currently lives with her cat, Miss Marple. Isabella also has other strong passions: traveling, watching movies and reading - a lot!

Library of Congress PCN Data

Sarah's Day in Kindergarten / Robin Wells

ISBN 978-1-68342-723-0 (hard cover)(alk. paper)
ISBN 978-1-68342-775-9 (soft cover)
ISBN 978-1-68342-827-5 (e-Book)
Library of Congress Control Number: 2017935438

Rourke Educational Media
Printed in the United States of America, North Mankato, Minnesota

© 2018 Rourke Educational Media

www.rourkeeducationalmedia.com

Edited by: Debra Ankiel
Art direction and layout by: Rhea Magaro-Wallace
Cover and interior Illustrations by: Isabella Grott